Pupunzel

by Maribeth Boelts

illustrated by Hollie Hibbert

Random House 🏠 New York

Once upon a time,
a mama dog had
six fat puppies.

They lived together
in the woods.

One day,
Mama Dog found
an overgrown garden.
The garden had
a plant called rapunzel.
Rapunzel was yummy!

Dear Parents:

Congratulations! Your child is taking the first steps on an exciting journey. The destination? Independent reading!

STEP INTO READING® will help your child get there. The program offers five steps to reading success. Each step includes fun stories and colorful art or photographs. In addition to original fiction and books with favorite characters, there are Step into Reading Non-Fiction Readers, Phonics Readers and Boxed Sets, Sticker Readers, and Comic Readers—a complete literacy program with something to interest every child.

Learning to Read, Step by Step!

Ready to Read   Preschool–Kindergarten
• big type and easy words • rhyme and rhythm • picture clues
For children who know the alphabet and are eager to begin reading.

Reading with Help   Preschool–Grade 1
• basic vocabulary • short sentences • simple stories
For children who recognize familiar words and sound out new words with help.

Reading on Your Own   Grades 1–3
• engaging characters • easy-to-follow plots • popular topics
For children who are ready to read on their own.

Reading Paragraphs   Grades 2–3
• challenging vocabulary • short paragraphs • exciting stories
For newly independent readers who read simple sentences with confidence.

Ready for Chapters   Grades 2–4
• chapters • longer paragraphs • full-color art
For children who want to take the plunge into chapter books but still like colorful pictures.

STEP INTO READING® is designed to give every child a successful reading experience. The grade levels are only guides; children will progress through the steps at their own speed, developing confidence in their reading. The F&P Text Level on the back cover serves as another tool to help you choose the right book for your child.

Remember, a lifetime love of reading starts with a single step!

To Deb, for bringing books
and young readers together
—M.B.

For my sister, Shandi Jan. Obviously.
—H.H.

Text copyright © 2016 by Maribeth Boelts
Cover art and interior illustrations copyright © 2016 by Hollie Hibbert

All rights reserved. Published in the United States by Random House Children's Books,
a division of Penguin Random House LLC, New York.

Step into Reading, Random House, and the Random House colophon are registered trademarks
of Penguin Random House LLC.

Visit us on the Web!
StepIntoReading.com
randomhousekids.com

Educators and librarians, for a variety of teaching tools, visit us at RHTeachersLibrarians.com

Library of Congress Cataloging-in-Publication Data
Names: Boelts, Maribeth, author. | Hibbert, Hollie, illustrator.
Title: Pupunzel / by Maribeth Boelts ; illustrated by Hollie Hibbert.
Description: New York : Random House, [2016] | Series: Step into reading.
Step 3 | Summary: Pupunzel is locked in a tower by a witch but the cocker spaniel puppy
and her family are determined to set things right in this twist on Rapunzel.
Identifiers: LCCN 2015038769 | ISBN 978-1-101-93449-4 (paperback) |
ISBN 978-1-101-93447-0 (hardcover library binding) | ISBN 978-1-101-93448-7 (ebook)
Subjects: | CYAC: Fairy tales. | Cocker spaniels—Fiction. | Dogs—Fiction. |
Animals—Infancy—Fiction. | BISAC: JUVENILE FICTION / Animals / Dogs. |
JUVENILE FICTION / Fairy Tales & Folklore / General. | JUVENILE FICTION /
Humorous Stories.
Classification: LCC PZ8.B6375 Pup 2016 | DDC [E]—dc23

Printed in the United States of America
10 9 8 7 6 5 4 3 2

This book has been officially leveled by using the F&P Text Level Gradient™ Leveling System.

Mama Dog looked around.
"This garden does not
belong to anyone," she said.
"I will pick some rapunzel
for my puppies."

But Mama Dog was wrong.
The garden belonged
to a witch.
Mama Dog picked a tiny bit
of rapunzel.

"This garden is mine!"
said the witch.
"You will pay for
what you have done!"

"I'm so sorry!"
said Mama Dog.
"What if I fetch
your slippers?"

But the witch did not

want her slippers.

She chose

one of the puppies instead.

"No!" cried Mama Dog.

"She is mine now!"

said the witch.

The witch named the puppy Pupunzel.
She locked her
in a tall tower,
far away.

Every day,
she brushed Pupunzel's fur
with a magic brush.
Pupunzel's fur grew longer
and longer.

When the witch visited,
she would shout,
"Pupunzel, Pupunzel,
let down your fur!"

Pupunzel threw
a long strand of fur
out the window.
The witch climbed up.

Pupunzel's family
searched for her everywhere.

They hiked over hills.

They bounded through brooks.

Deep in the woods,
they heard barking.
They followed the sound
to the tower.

"Woof!" said Mama Dog.
"Woof! Woof! Woof!"
said the brothers and sisters.
Pupunzel raced
to the window.

She threw down her fur,

and they all climbed up.

"Now we can be together!"

said Mama Dog.

"I will need vines
to make a rope,"
said Pupunzel.
"Then I can climb down
from the tower.
We will all run away."

Pupunzel told Mama Dog
where to find strong vines.
"Look in the woods," she said.
"But be careful."

Pupunzel's family

climbed down from the tower.

They crept into the woods

and bit off vines

with their strong teeth.

That night,
they brought the vines
to Pupunzel.

"The rope is almost done!"

said Pupunzel.

"Bring two more vines

tomorrow."

Off they went.

The witch had been spying.

She flew to the tower.

"Pupunzel, Pupunzel,
let down your fur!"
she shouted.

The witch climbed up
and saw the rope
Pupunzel was making.

"Bad dog!" the witch said.

She snipped off

Pupunzel's long golden fur.

She flew Pupunzel
to the woods
and left her there.

The next morning,
Pupunzel's family came
to the tower.
The witch was waiting,
ready to play a trick.

The witch dangled
Pupunzel's fur
out the window.
The family climbed up.

The witch laughed.

"Pupunzel is gone," she said.

"You will be trapped

in the tower forever."

Back in the woods,

Pupunzel was lost.

She had to get back

to the tower.

But how would she find

her way?

Just then,
Pupunzel remembered
her nose.

The witch smelled like
a pickle inside
an old, wet shoe.

Pupunzel put her nose
to the ground.

She would follow the smell
right back to the tower!

Sniff, sniff, sniff.

Pupunzel sniffed as she ran.

She sniffed as she
hiked over hills.

She sniffed as she
bounded through brooks.

The yucky smell
led her to the tower!
"Woof!" she barked.

Mama Dog and

the brothers and sisters

looked out the window.

"I will save you!"

said Pupunzel.

But the witch was hiding.

She jumped out
to catch Pupunzel.
"Now you will ALL be mine!"
she said.

Pupunzel had one last idea.
She jumped up on the witch
and knocked her down.
She covered the witch's face
with sloppy dog kisses.

Suddenly,

the witch began to twitch.

She began to shake.

Presto!

The witch turned into

a princess!

The princess had been

under a spell all along!

The spell was broken

by the kiss of a brave dog.

The princess

wrapped her arms

around Pupunzel.

"How can I ever thank you?"

she said.

Pupunzel ran to the tower.

She barked and barked.

"We must rescue your family!"

said the princess.

The princess called

the royal fire brigade.

The firefighters brought
a long ladder.
One by one,
Pupunzel's family
were rescued.
There was happy dancing
and prancing.
There was joyful chasing
and racing.

After that,
Pupunzel and her family
got the royal treatment.
And they all lived
happily ever after!